This book belongs to:

....

HODDER CHILDREN'S BOOKS

First published in Great Britain in 2015 by Hodder and Stoughton
This paperback edition published in 2016
Copyright © Pat Hutchins, 2015
The moral rights of the author and illustrator have been asserted.
All rights reserved.

A CIP catalogue record of this book
is available from the British Library.

ISBN: 978 1 444 91829 8
10 9 8 7 6 5 4 3 2 1

Printed and bound in China.

Hodder Children's Books
An imprint of Hachette Children's Group
Part of Hodder and Stoughton
Carmelite House
50 Victoria Embankment
London EC4Y 0DZ

An Hachette UK Company
www.hachette.co.uk
www.hachettechildrens.co.uk

Where, Oh Where, is Rosie's Chick?

Pat Hutchins

For Susan,
who hatched Rosie,
and Anne,
who hatched Rosie's chick.

- P.H.

Hooray!
Rosie the hen
has laid
an egg.

And, at last, her egg is hatching...

But, oh no!

Where is little baby chick?

Rosie looked under the hen house,

but little baby chick wasn't there.

She looked in the basket,
but little baby chick wasn't there.

She looked behind the wheelbarrow,
but little baby chick wasn't there either.

She looked across the fields,

but she still couldn't find little baby chick!

She looked through the straw,
but little baby chick wasn't there either.

Where, oh where,
is little baby chick?

BEHIND YOU!

Then Rosie and her little
baby chick went for a walk...

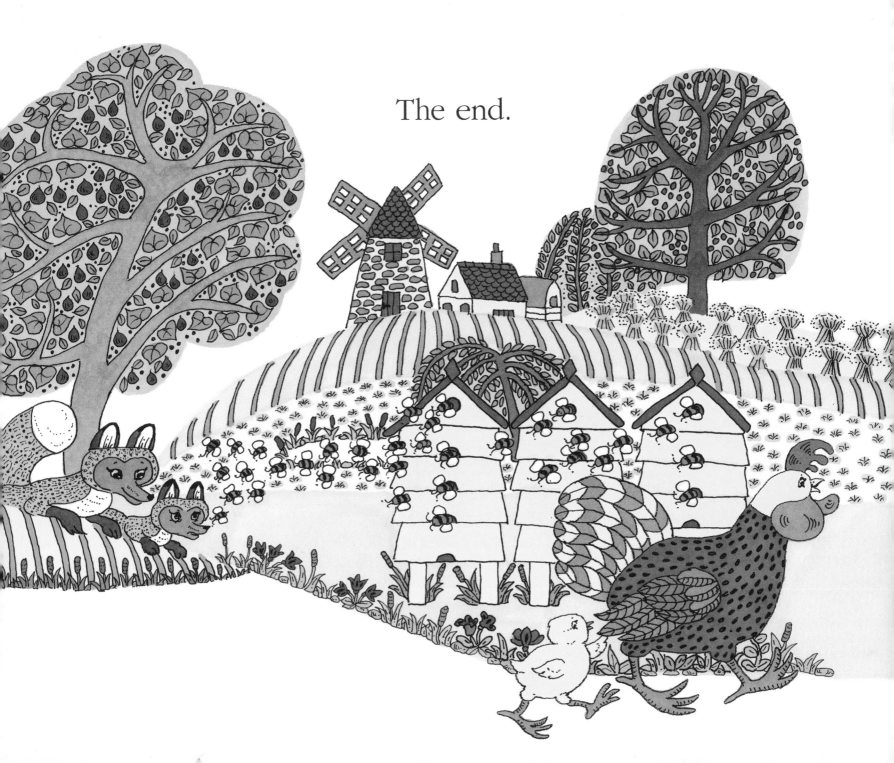

The end.

Dear Girls and Boys,

I hope you like this new story about Rosie and her little baby chick.

When I was young I had friends who had a pet hen called Rosie, and when I grew up I wrote a book about her. Rosie's Walk was my very first picture book.

I always thought - what if Rosie had a chick? Well, here she is.

I hope you enjoy your walk with Rosie and her little baby chick.

With love,

Pat x

Praise for *Rosie's Walk*:

"A sunny, slapstick silent comedy."
NEW YORK TIMES

"The pictures tell an action-packed story full of drama and surprise."
JULIA ECCLESHERE, GUARDIAN

"The highly patterned red, orange and yellow graphics are as fresh and funny as they were in 1968 and will make 2-4s howl with laughter."
THE TIMES

"All young children will enjoy the tale of Rosie the hen and her walk around the farm followed by a hungry but thankfully hapless fox."
SUNDAY EXPRESS

"A delightful tale from a celebrated author."
NURSERY EDUCATION

"The perfect picture book for teaching children to read."
BOOKS FOR KEEPS